בס"ד

This book belongs to: לה׳ הארץ ומלואה

Please read it to me!

Yossi and Laibel Hot On The Trail

For my mother, who will never really be alone on her trail through life. D.R.

For my children - Debby & Maxine, and grandchildren Jackie & Danny. N.N.

First Edition – Kislev 5751 / November 1991
Second Impression – Cheshvan 5757 / October 1996
Third Impression – Nissan 5760 / April 2000
Fourth Impression – Shevat 5762 / January 2002

ISBN: 0-922613-47-8
LCCN: 94-103747

HACHAI PUBLISHING
Brooklyn, N.Y. 11218
Tel: 718-633-0100 Fax: 718-633-0103
www.hachai.com   info@hachai.com

Printed in China

YOSSI AND LAIBEL
HOT ON THE TRAIL

It was scorching and dry on that long summer day
Too hot to ride bikes and too hot to play.
Not a cloud in the sky, not a breeze in the air
So Laibel and Yossi just lounged on a chair.

They sat back to back, drinking cold lemonade
And sucking the ice on the porch in the shade.
But as the boys' eyelids drooped over their eyes
Came the sound of small sniffles and sad little cries.

Yossi blinked, rubbed his eyes, and sat up in his chair.
"What's the matter?" he called out. "What's wrong over there?"
A small girl in tears stood behind their front bush,
Her little doll carriage too broken to push.

"Come on," Yossi shouted to his older brother,
"Let's fix it and send the girl home to her mother!"

"You're kidding," said Laibel. "It's much, much too hot!
Why should I leave my chair and my nice shady spot?
I need ice and cold drinks, and I simply can't budge."
Then Yossi's sharp elbow gave Laibel a nudge.

"You know there's a *mitzvah* to help every Jew
No matter what and no matter who
With any size problem or any request!
This will just take a minute and then you can rest."

"Well okay," agreed Laibel, "but after one minute,
It's back to my chair and I'm sitting down in it!"

The poor little carriage was tipped on its side
One wheel was off, and it just wouldn't ride.
The boys looked around it, beside and behind it
But one screw was missing, and they couldn't find it.

Yossi said to the girl, "Wait right here — please do,
While my brother and I go to buy a new screw."
"Now hold on," said Laibel. "You can't go alone
Our parents won't let you, and I'm staying home!"

"No, you're not," answered Yossi,
"We'll see this thing through,

Because there's a *mitzvah* to help every Jew.
No matter what and no matter who!"
And Yossi set off in a rush down the street
With Laibel behind him, dragging his feet.

The big hardware store was empty that day;
The boys found the screw and went over to pay.
When the store owner said, "Boys, that screw is for free
If you'll just find the time to do something for me.
Today I left home in this terrible heat
Forgetting my lunch box, and now I can't eat.
Would you please go next door to the kosher bakery
And buy some brown bread and three muffins for me?"

Yossi said, "We can go if my brother wants to."
"Oh, great," muttered Laibel, "what else can I do
When I know there's a *mitzvah* to help every Jew
No matter what and no matter who?"

So they set off at once to the bakery shop
With the screw in a bag and the money on top.

The bakery felt like an oven inside
Though the doors and the windows were all opened wide.
The baker could barely stand up on his feet
Or take a deep breath in the stifling heat.

Yossi bought the food and then asked the poor man,
"Excuse me, Mr. Baker, don't you have a fan?"

"Well, I did," wheezed the baker, "but now it won't run
And my old friend the butcher said he'd give me one
But at this busy time I just can't leave my store . . ."
And he wiped his red face, and he stared at the floor.

Yossi and Laibel just looked at each other;
Then Laibel grinned down at his little brother.
"Don't say it, Yossi, I know what we'll do,
Because there's a *mitzvah* to help every Jew
No matter what and no matter who.
We'll bring back that fan in a minute or two!"

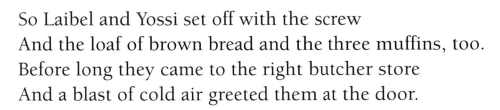

So Laibel and Yossi set off with the screw
And the loaf of brown bread and the three muffins, too.
Before long they came to the right butcher store
And a blast of cold air greeted them at the door.

From the back of the store came a screech and a scream
But where was the butcher? Nowhere to be seen.

Just two children covered from faces to feet
With splatters of goo and chunks of red meat.

"Sorry, boys," said the butcher, "but my wife's away
And I'm watching my two-year-old twins for the day.
They have nothing to play with — no puzzle or ball,
So I can't get any work done here at all!"

"Well, sir," began Laibel, "we came for the fan,
But we'd both like to help you out if we can.
Just because there's a *mitzvah* to help every Jew
No matter what and no matter who.
We'll go to the toy store and look for some toys,
Something that's fun for your little twin boys."

And off went those two with a *mitzvah* to do
Holding fan, brown bread, muffins, and one little screw.

At the toy counter they asked for box
Of crayons, two puzzles, a ball, and some blocks.
The lady said, "Those things are on the third shelf.
I'm afraid that today you must get them yourself.
My shoelaces tore and I've nothing to use
In place of the laces to tie up my shoes."

Laibel paid for the toys and then said, "Never fear,
I know of a shoe store that's right around here.
We'll run there and get you a new pair of laces."
The lady smiled down at their hot, tired faces.
"Don't you boys have anything else you must do?"
"That's okay," answered Yossi, "we want to help you,
Just because there's a *mitzvah* to help every Jew
No matter what and no matter who!"

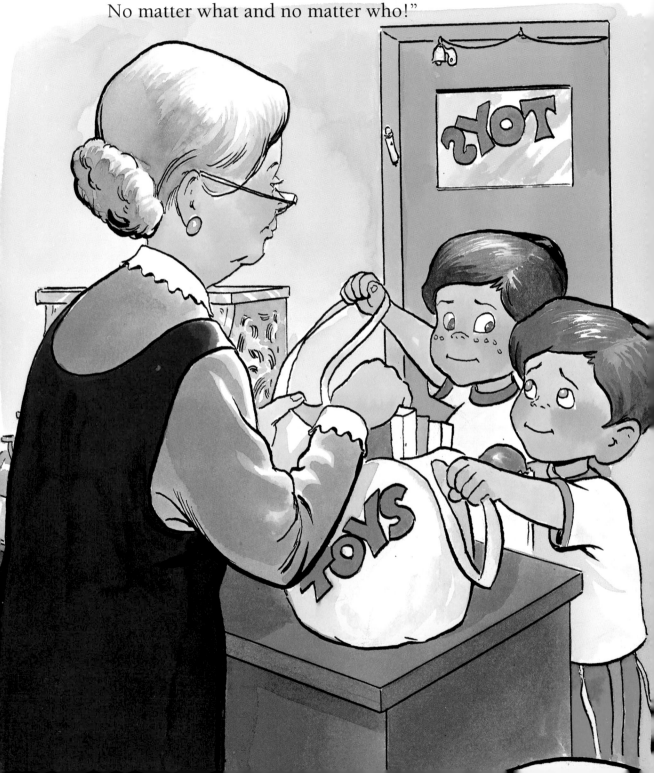

So Yossi and Laibel were soon on their way
With the size of the laces, some money to pay,
The crayons, two puzzles, some blocks and a ball,
The fan, loaf of bread, muffins, small screw and all!

They came to the shoe store and picked the right pack
Of laces for ladies' shoes right off the rack.
As they paid him, the shoemaker asked with a frown,
"Have you boys been walking all through the town?
Perhaps you have seen my granddaughter near here.
She's been gone for an hour and I really fear
That she's lost or she's hurt, and I really can't wait
So I'm going to search before it gets late."

Laibel was worried and Yossi was, too.
"What does she look like? We'll find her for you.
Because there's a *mitzvah* to help every Jew
No matter what and no matter who!"

"Well," said the shoemaker, "She's really quite small,
And she's pushing a toy carriage with her best doll!"

The boys began laughing till tears filled their eyes
And the shoemaker stared at them both in surprise.
Laibel said, "Mr. Shoemaker, please do not worry,
We'll bring your granddaughter back in a hurry.
We know where she is and just why she is late —
I'm afraid it's our fault for making her wait!"

So Yossi and Laibel started to run
Up again, back again, in the hot sun.
In again, out again, right through each door
Dashing about again into each store.

Shoelaces for the one selling the toys
Toys for the butcher's two little boys
Fan for the baker to cool off the heat
Bread for the hardware store owner to eat.

Then they ran home with that one little screw
And fixed up the doll carriage as good as new.
They told the girl, "Grandfather's waiting for you!
We'll walk you right to him, that's just what we'll do,
Because there's a *mitzvah* to help every Jew
No matter what and no matter who!"

When the boys came back home, they found warm lemonade
The ice cubes had melted, there was no more shade
The chairs were all sticky and hot from the sun.
Then their mother came out and looked at each one.

"Oh, boys," she said, "you seem so tired and hot
I think I can fix that — just look what I've got."
Their mother unrolled the long garden hose
And sprinkled them both on the grass in their clothes.

Soon their father drove up and said, "What a hot day!"
Look what I brought home for you on my way
Two ice cream cones with four flavors each
Chocolate, strawberry, vanilla, and peach!"

Then Laibel said, "Yossi, I see it is true
That sometime, someone will be sure to help you

If you do your best to help every Jew
No matter what and no matter who!"

The End